A TOP SECRET MESSAGE

Hi, I'm Matt, and I have a superpower.

Until recently I was just ordinary – going to school, having a laugh with my mates, liking a girl called Emma who liked me too – but as a friend. I wanted it to be more.

Then, one fateful day, I visited an old lady called Mrs Jameson. She was supposed to be very difficult and didn't get along with anyone. Except, would you believe, me. Soon I was visiting her every day and when she died she left me a crystal, which she had always worn around her neck.

There was a note from her too, saying no one else can ever know how special the crystal is. Only me.

And one day I discovered the crystal's incredible power.

IT CAN READ MINDS …

MindReader
SUPERHERO

Pete Johnson

award

ISBN 978-1-78270-304-4

Cover design by Patrick Knowles
Illustrations by Anthony Smith

Text copyright © 2018 Pete Johnson
This edition copyright © Award Publications Limited

First published by Award Publications Limited 2018

Published by Award Publications Limited,
The Old Riding School, Welbeck, Worksop, S80 3LR

www.awardpublications.co.uk

18 1

Printed in the United Kingdom

*This book is dedicated to my dogs –
past and present – who all inspired
me when creating Scampi.*

Chapter One

Losing the Crystal

It's me, Matt, again. Up to a few weeks ago I was just an ordinary boy. Now I have a strange, eerie *SUPERPOWER*. Maybe you have read about it and how my whole life changed because of a crystal.

The crystal belonged to Mrs Jameson, an old lady I came to know very well. She always wore this crystal round her neck, which fascinated me, perhaps because there were flashes of so many colours in it.

After she died, Mrs Jameson left the crystal to me with a highly mysterious note. She said no one else must discover just how special the crystal was – only me.

It took a while to figure out the crystal's secret, but when I did ...

IT CAN READ MINDS. No, it really can.

How does it work? Let me give you a quick demo. So you walk past me and I'm keen to know what you're thinking. All I have to do is move the crystal slightly in your direction, wait a few moments for it to warm up, then I'll hear your every thought exactly as if you were whispering them right in my ear.

And I can go on earwigging until the crystal becomes too hot to hold. Then I let it cool down before I start again.

And it doesn't matter how far away you are from me. So you could be up one end of a field and I could be at the other. I can still listen in – or 'tune in', as I prefer to call it – to you.

By the way, if you're sitting in your house, you're still not safe from me. Oh no. The crystal can eavesdrop through glass too.

Does this all sound a bit weird to you, even a bit spooky? Trust me, you'll soon get used to it.

And it's also totally brilliant, isn't it?

I will admit the crystal has caused me a lot of hassle, especially with Emma, my best mate. That's why I decided I would never use the crystal on friends again.

And I actually thought I'd learnt all I needed to know about my crystal. But I so hadn't. And lately, some truly incredible things have happened that I'd really like to tell you about.

It all started when I did something deeply shaming. I LOST MY CRYSTAL.

I was at Finn's party.

Maybe you haven't met Finn before? You're so lucky. I can describe him to you in three words – spoilt, sneaky, slimy.

So why on earth was I going to his party? Well, everyone else was going, and I guess I didn't want to miss out, even though I knew it would depress me greatly to observe exactly how big Finn's house was and how much money was wasted on him.

Still, the party was OK-ish – tons of food, anyhow. Finn, of course, was just bursting with smugness and spent the whole time showing off.

So, actually, did his parents.

His mum was wearing these trendy leather trousers and platform shoes. She even had a nose ring. I saw Emma staring at her and, just for a laugh, I broke my rule of not tuning in to friends. And Emma was thinking:

She's too old and wrinkly to be wearing a nose ring. She just looks ridiculous.

I turned to Emma. "Don't you think Finn's mum is too old and wrinkly to be wearing an earring in her nose? She just looks ridiculous."

Emma gave a little gasp on hearing me repeat her thoughts, but then she quickly said, "Oh that is so cruel, Matt. I think she looks all right." I just grinned to myself.

Later, we played Murder in the Dark. Of course, there were masses of places to hide. I hid under the stairs. I knew someone was nearby. I could hear him wheezing softly. It sounded exactly like Finn. I decided to check and reached out for my crystal. I always keep it on my belt. Only it wasn't there. It must have fallen off!

Well, I was frantic. I forgot all about the game. I searched everywhere for it. Emma soon joined in. And Finn pretended to hunt for it. "I'm sure it will turn up, Spud." (That's my nickname because my nose looks a bit like a potato. Hardly anyone calls me that now, except him, of course.) But I had the strangest feeling Finn knew far more than he was letting on.

You see, Finn doesn't like me much. (He does like Emma, but that's another story.) So he'd enjoy hiding my crystal and then watching me sweat as I searched everywhere for it.

Finally, Emma said, "Don't worry, I'll buy you another crystal when I get my birthday money."

How could I tell her my crystal was irreplaceable and priceless?

Some of us were sleeping over. Emma was sharing a room with two other girls and I was with a mate called Cameron.

The bedroom was very hot. Finn's family could obviously afford to leave the heating on all night. Cameron fell asleep almost at once. Normally, I'd have drifted off to sleep too, but that night I tossed and turned. Where on earth was my crystal?

I was more certain than ever that Finn knew where it was. His room was next to mine. Should I just barge in there and interrogate him?

And then I heard something that made me sit right up in bed.

"Go away! Just leave me alone!" Someone was yelling.

It was Finn.

Chapter Two

The Whispering Ghosts

Normally, I wouldn't have lifted a fingernail to help Finn. But there was something about that cry. It sounded desperate. And I seemed to have been the only one who'd heard him. I scrambled out of bed and crept next door.

Finn was standing right by the door. He made me jump and his gross, bright-red pyjamas that had his initials on the top pocket made me want to vomit!

"What's the matter with you?" I demanded.

What made everything even weirder was that he didn't answer. He just looked as if he'd been turned to stone – if only.

Then, all at once, he seemed to notice me, and very slowly turned his face in my direction. It was covered in sweat. "I've just seen a ghost," he informed me in a low croak.

I'd have burst out laughing except he looked deathly pale and his right hand was actually shaking.

"It was here in my bedroom," he hissed, "whispering at me."

"Quite a chatty ghost then," I said.

"It was sort of whispering but very loudly, if you know what I mean?"

"No, I haven't a clue," I said cheerfully. By now I was thinking of my crystal. Yet, how could it be mixed up in all this? Unless Finn had fallen asleep holding it.

"I don't suppose you heard anything?" asked Finn.

"Only you squealing like a terrified piglet."

"I don't think you realise what has happened. A ghost has started haunting me."

"Rubbish, ghosts have got much better taste."

Then Finn's parents tore in. They were both in matching initialled bright-red pyjamas too. The three of them looked as if they'd escaped from the Starship Enterprise.

"We thought we'd heard you," gushed his mum. "Tell us exactly what happened, love." They perched either side of him on his bed. Finn's bottom lip started to wobble. Big baby.

In hushed tones, Finn told them about his ghostly visitor, while I was growing more and more sceptical. I prowled around his bedroom ,searching for my crystal. I was convinced it was here somewhere. Then his parents, oozing concern, took Finn downstairs for 'a sugary drink to calm his nerves'.

I was about to leave when a voice hissed loudly:

I'm not going to hang around. That wind's got a real sting of winter in it.

It was as if someone was whispering through a loud hailer at me. Only, of course, the room was completely empty. So was it Finn's talkative ghost or … I drew back the thick curtains. A man in a heavy, dark coat was walking briskly down the road. Was it his thoughts I'd just heard? But how? The crystal only worked when someone was holding it, didn't it?

Then I glanced down and there was my crystal, wedged down behind the radiator. My heart beat excitedly.

So Finn had found my crystal, exactly as I'd suspected, and then hidden it behind his radiator. Later, he'd pretended to look for it. Talk about mean. And would I ever have got it back from him? I doubted it. He knew it meant a lot to me. So he had to have it. That's Finn for you.

I bent down to grab it, and then nearly dropped it again. My crystal was scorching hot. I touched the radiator. That was boiling too.

The crystal must have caught the heat from the radiator. Then as it got hotter, it started picking up people's thoughts through the window just above it. The hotter it got, the louder it was, beaming these thoughts into Finn's bedroom in full stereosonic sound. How freaky was that? No wonder he was so terrified.

I heard footsteps coming up the stairs. I was about to rush out with my crystal but then an idea grew inside me. A very wicked idea, which made me want to laugh out loud.

I hastily returned the crystal to its place behind the radiator, exactly as I'd found it, tilted slightly towards the window.

I crept back to my room. I waited for Finn's parents to leave. They were ages. I heard them reassuring Finn that he wouldn't have any more bad dreams. I grinned to myself. That's what they thought. At last they returned to their own room.

I started to get dressed. Suddenly, I stopped. But I didn't need to go outside, did I? I could just …

I opened the window and stuck my head out as far as it would go. Would the crystal pick up my thoughts? I was about to find out. So was Finn.

But I was interrupted by a sleepy voice demanding, "Matt, what on earth are you doing?"

I turned round. "Just getting a breath of

fresh air."

"But it's the middle of the night – and it's freezing."

"The trouble is, I've got faulty sinuses."

"What?"

"And I have to clean them regularly or they get all clogged up with stale snot—"

"Ugh! Too much information," interrupted Cameron.

I pushed my head out again and started breathing through my nose very loudly.

"You have got some disgusting habits," muttered Cameron.

I carried on with my deep breathing, thinking:

Tonight, Finn, you stole something, a crystal, which belongs to Matthew. That was very wrong of you. I am Matthew's guardian angel and I will send ghostly people to haunt you forever unless you return it to its rightful owner. But hurry up, Finn, you haven't got long.

For good measure, I added:

*Your parents can't save you this time ...
No one can ... So beware ... Beware!*

"Haven't you finished yet?" Cameron was sitting up in bed watching me now.

"Yeah, my sinuses are completely declogged and snot free now."

"I'm so relieved," he murmured.

I closed the window. And I'd just got back into bed when I heard footsteps.

"Pretend to be asleep," I hissed at Cameron.

"What's going on now?" he muttered, but he did as I'd asked.

The bedroom door opened. It was Finn. He crept towards me. I heard a tiny chink as he placed something on the little bedside table.

I half-opened my eyes. It was my crystal. Its colours shone in the darkness. Finn tiptoed out again, closing the bedroom door quietly behind him.

Cameron asked, "What did Finn just do?"

"I think he found my crystal for me."

"Weird time to bring it back."

"But then Finn's a weird guy. Still, better late

than never. Night."

I gazed down at the crystal now nestling in my hand.

I was determined I'd never lose it again.

Chapter Three

In Trouble

The following night, when everyone in my house was asleep, I wrote up what had happened. I have a special exercise book: *THE THIRD EAR* (my code name for the crystal).

This is what I wrote:

AMAZING DISCOVERY. The Third Ear works when put behind a radiator and allowed to get hot. As it gets hotter, the whispering becomes much louder.

IMPORTANT. When you hold the Third Ear, only you can pick up the thoughts. But if it is behind a boiling radiator, anyone in the room can 'overhear' what is being thought.

More soon.

I was so excited about all this that I did something stupid.

My family don't usually keep the heating on at night. But we were having such a cold snap, my mum decided, just this once, she would leave it on. So I couldn't resist jamming my crystal at the back of the radiator and then waiting to overhear the thoughts of whoever walked past my window.

Only no one walked past, and so I fell asleep. Later, I jumped awake. At first I thought someone was in my room. In a way, someone was. This man was hissing away in the darkness about why he hated his cousin.

To be honest, he scared me out of my wits. And the voice was so loud, I didn't like it at all. I must move the crystal right now. But then a shadow stepped towards me, and became my mum.

"Matthew, what on earth are you listening

to? And why on earth are you letting your radio blare out like that?"

Of course, what my mum had heard wasn't anything to do with the radio.

"Sorry, Mum, I just couldn't sleep."

"Do you know what time it is? I've got such a lot to do tomorrow, with your dad away and all."

"I've switched it off now, Mum."

She huffed a bit more and turned to go. Then, to my complete horror, a voice hissed:

I'm sick of her going on at me for nothing. She's a real pain these days.

Mum was back in my room in an instant, glaring furiously at me. "What did you just say? How dare you be so rude, Matthew. And I didn't have a go at you for nothing."

Before I could reply, this girl's voice chimed in:

Why can't she shut her face?

23

"What did you say, Matt?"

"Erm ... well," I began, desperately searching for a way out of this one. "It was only a joke."

"A joke?" thundered Mum. "And you think you can get away with it by putting on those silly voices? I can tell you, they are not funny at all."

"Sorry, Mum."

"Is the performance over now?"

"It really is," I cried, terrified the crystal was going to pick up another passer-by's thoughts. So I buried myself down in the bed. "So sleepy," and then started snoring very enthusiastically.

The very second Mum left, I was out of bed and yanking my crystal away from the radiator. Only it was so hot, I dropped it on the carpet. I had to scoop it up in tissue and then leave it on the little table by my bed. I was incredibly angry with myself. I'd been a real banana-brain tonight.

Next morning at breakfast, the atmosphere was distinctly chilly. This was a shame, as lately Mum and I had been getting on well. I was mad keen to have a dog. Only Mum wasn't. But I'd started to talk her round, and just last night she and I had chatted about adopting a dog from the local Animal Rescue Centre. Some chance now.

Before I went to school, I sped off to the local sweet shop. The elderly couple who owned it — the Kossoffs — had been away. Mr Kossoff had been pretty ill and needed a long convalescence. And the lady who'd been looking after the shop for them had totally ruined the atmosphere.

You'd just walk in and she'd snap, "Yes, what do you want then?" in a really unfriendly way. But now the Kossoffs were back and I looked forward to the shop returning to its old cosy ways.

I got a shock when I arrived though. Mr and Mrs Kossoff were creaking about on their knees, picking up stuff that was scattered right across the floor.

Mr Kossoff peered up anxiously as the shop bell clanged, then he saw me and relaxed. "Ah, here's one of our very favourite customers." He was a small, silver-haired man with a matching toothbrush moustache. As usual, he was dressed in a suit with a rose poking out of his jacket buttonhole.

"Yes, wonderful to see you again, Matt." Mrs Kossoff was very small – barely any taller than me – but always busy and bustling about. "And sorry about the mess."

"Have you had an earthquake in here or something?" I asked.

Mr Kossoff gave a short laugh and then said quickly. "A little accident … I'm so clumsy. And on my first week back as well! Should sack myself really." He gave another odd laugh.

I gazed at him and Mrs Kossoff, who were both looking distinctly out of breath.

"How about if I give you a hand to pick up the rest and you sling it on the shelves?" I suggested.

"Oh no—" began Mr Kossoff.

But Mrs Kossoff interrupted, "That's very kind of you, Matt." So I bounced about, and afterwards they insisted I accept a free bar of chocolate as a thank-you. They were being extremely cheerful, but something was very wrong. Never in a million years had Mr Kossoff accidentally flung half the contents of the shop about.

No, someone had burst in and done it. I was sure of that.

I wanted to help the Kossoffs, but they just didn't want to talk about it, and soon the shop was filling up with customers. I'd be back though.

In fact, I'd planned to visit the shop with Emma again after school. But she was too excited about Finn's 'early birthday present'. She waved her left hand at me. On it were two watches – her old one and, totally outclassing it, a dazzlingly new chunky diver's watch, complete with stopwatch button and an alarm and … but you get the idea.

"I wasn't expecting a present like this," cried Emma. "He can't spend all this money on me!"

"I'll give it back to him if you like," I suggested hopefully.

Emma's voice fell. "The thing is, I do need a new watch and he probably can't take it back now anyway."

I didn't say another word about it. I was too eaten up with jealousy and frustration. I could never compete with a present like that. Trust

Finn to throw his money about. And I knew why he was doing it too. He badly wanted to go out with Emma.

We'd always been rivals where she was concerned. I'd wanted to go out with Emma for yonks. But I'd never done anything about it, as I wasn't at all sure if Emma liked me enough.

IF ONLY I KNEW.

Well. There are two ways I can find out.

Ask Emma out.

Or use my crystal on her.

Yet, hadn't I made a promise never to use my crystal on friends? You're right, I have.

BUT, if I discover Emma doesn't fancy me, well I won't go any further, saving not only me from a massively embarrassing scene, but Emma too.

You could say I would be doing Emma a favour.

Well, you could.

Chapter Four

Helping Emma

On Friday, after school, I decided to discover –
with the help of my trusty crystal – what my
chances were with Emma.

There was only one place private enough for
this – the oak tree in the wood, just a stone's
throw away from Emma's house.

Emma and I love climbing trees. The huge old
oak tree was our favourite because it was quite
easy to climb. There was even a hole in the trunk
where you could lift yourself up. And best of all,
about halfway up, it had a wide, comfortable
branch that was just right for sitting on. So in

29

the summer, Emma and I would sit there for hours, telling spooky stories and talking about things. There was also an epic view, stretching right across our village and the town beyond.

But now it was the beginning of October and Emma looked stunned when I suggested climbing our oak tree.

"Be a bit cold, won't it?" she said.

"We've got coats on."

She grinned. "Why not then?"

Climbing up a tree in a coat and scarf is actually quite hard. Our sleeves kept catching on the branches, so we were stopping all the time to disentangle ourselves.

"This is a bit like swimming with your clothes on," cried Emma.

"Can't say I've ever tried that," I replied.

We picked our way to the branch, settled ourselves, and then Emma said, "So what do you want to talk about?"

"Well, nothing really."

"Yes you do. Come on – and hurry up. It's freezing."

Well, I knew I couldn't ask her outright if she

liked me. I had to build up to it. So I said, "I just wanted to chat about the cinema."

"The cinema!" she echoed.

"Yeah. I just wondered what actors you like these days." My crystal was pointed at her and my hands were all tingly with excitement.

So Emma rattled on about what movie stars she liked, while the crystal heard:

I've got a horrible feeling I know why Matt is asking me these questions. I really hope I'm wrong.

A cold fever settled in my stomach. This sounded horribly unpromising. But I pressed on. "Do you prefer guys with blond hair or dark hair?" (I've got black hair in case you're interested, which you're not.)

She gabbled something about how, "It depended on the rest of the guy's face." But I was too busy listening to my crystal:

I'm going to pretend I don't know what this is leading up to. But I do. I've always dreaded this moment. Matt's going to ask me out, isn't he?

Chills raced up and down my spine now. There wasn't much point in asking any more questions as I knew the outcome already – no sale.

But then I overheard:

Of course, I do think Matt is fit.

Immediately, a great big smile plastered itself across my face.

"What are you smiling at?" asked Emma.

"Nothing." I started to giggle. Emma thinks I'm fit. I could smile for a week.

"Come on, tell me," said Emma.

"No, I just feel dead good, that's all," I said. But I couldn't get rid of that goofy smile.

"You were saying why you don't like boys with blonde streaks."

She carried on talking while the crystal overheard:

Matt's behaving very oddly tonight. But he mustn't ask me out, because if we go out together and then break up ... why, we'll end up nowhere. And I'll have lost my best friend. I can't risk that. Besides, tonight couldn't be a worse time – not when I'm so worried and upset. I'm surprised Matt hasn't noticed.

"You're worried about something, aren't you, Emma?" I asked.

She started. And for the first time I noticed how pale and washed-out she looked.

"If anyone realised, I knew it would be you," she said. "There's just a terrible atmosphere in my house at the moment." She stared out at the thousands of roofs and aerials below us. "My parents keep whispering in corners. Either they're about to get divorced or it's to do with me. I know they're cross about all my low marks at school. So I wouldn't be surprised if they're plotting to send me away to another school."

I sat up. "They mustn't do that."

"I just wish they'd tell me what's wrong. But

they won't – they keep pretending everything's fine – and it's really doing my head in."

"I'm not surprised."

Right then, I decided I'd solve this mystery for Emma. Well, with the help of the crystal, I would. I felt a bit like those knights in ancient tales who, before they can win the hand of the girl, have to perform a daring task, like fighting a fire-breathing dragon.

I performed my daring task on Saturday afternoon. I was sitting inside the kitchen with Emma and her pet dog, Bess. Her dad was out in the garden, vigorously brushing up some of the autumn leaves.

Emma was asking me about the history homework. She was anxious to do it right. I stood by the window talking to her, but I had my crystal trained on Emma's dad. So it was like trying to listen to two different conversations at once. Takes a certain amount of skill, actually. Especially as people don't often think in sentences. If they're very angry and upset, they just splutter out the odd word. That's exactly what happened with Emma's dad. So it took a while to work out what was bugging him.

But at last, I sussed it. And I couldn't wait to tell Emma. So later that afternoon when we were taking Bess for a walk, I blurted out, "I wonder if your dad's got worries at work. A lot of people do these days, you know. Maybe he's on a shortlist of six, four of whom will lose their jobs because of …" I repeated the word I'd overheard from Emma's dad, "restructuring."

"No, it's not that," said Emma. "My dad's job is totally secure."

"I wouldn't be so sure," I said. "Take it from me," I added mysteriously.

Having reassured Emma (I hope), I looked in on the Kossoffs. And they were only talking about retiring!

"But you've just got back," I said.

"And we are already finding it a bit much," said Mr Kossoff.

"We are very decrepit you know," added Mrs Kossoff, smiling weakly.

"But without you two, this shop is nothing,"

I began. Then I had a flash of inspiration. "I've got it," I cried excitedly. "I'll help you out. I can be here before school starts and every evening and through the weekends too and you needn't worry about paying me – just fling me the odd choc-chip. Now is that a tempting offer or what?"

They started chuckling away as if I'd said something hilarious. I was a bit insulted, actually.

"I am actually totally serious," I said indignantly.

"We know you are," said Mr Kossoff, wiping his eyes. "And we will miss you and all our friends so much ..."

"But it's time for us to go," cut in his wife, briskly. "And that's it."

I knew there was something the Kossoff's weren't telling me. Something really important. And it was so frustrating. But with the help of my crystal, I was determined to find out what it was. But then I received a text from Emma. She wanted to see me urgently – usual place.

I sped to the wood where she was waiting for me.

"Anything wrong?" I asked.

She smiled. "Let's go tree-climbing again."

It had rained earlier and the branches were wet and slimy and difficult to grip properly. We clambered up to our spot.

Then Emma exclaimed, "I can't believe it, but you were totally right. I asked my dad outright if he was worried about losing his job. He looked totally stunned. Then Mum came in and they both told me about this – and it was exactly the word you used too – restructuring.

"Dad's certain he's for the chop. He said he and Mum hadn't told me as there was no sense in worrying me as well. If they'd only realised …" She smiled. "But what I don't get, Matt, is how you knew. You were only in our house for about half an hour, but you worked it all out. You're so clever."

I stroked my chin thoughtfully. "That's very true."

"But how did you?" she persisted.

"A lucky guess – I guess." I was keen to change the subject now.

"But it's uncanny. I mean, he's on a shortlist

of six and four of them will lose their jobs. Exactly as you said."

I realised I'd given Emma far too many details. I shifted uneasily. "What can I say, I'm a genius."

But Emma went on looking very puzzled. So I added, "Plus, it happened to this uncle of mine."

"What uncle?"

"Raymond, Uncle Raymond." It was the first name that popped into my head. Don't ask why.

"I've never heard you mention him."

"Haven't you?"

"No," she said firmly.

"Well, that's because he's not very interesting. I don't see him much. I just know he was on a shortlist and nearly lost his job. But in the end, he didn't."

"So where did he work?"

"Where? Erm, Birmingham. In this factory."

"Does he still work there?"

"Yeah, I suppose so. I don't check up on him every day – we're not exactly best buddies."

"And you've visited him in Birmingham?" This was turning into an interrogation.

"Once or twice … millions of light years ago now." Then I hastily started talking about much more important things, like how I could persuade my mum to get a dog.

Grey darkness was rising up like smoke now, blotting out our marvellous view. A sparrow came bombing towards the oak tree, discovered us roosting there, and started flapping like mad before it shot away again.

"Poor thing, discovering us in its house," said Emma.

I was about to reply, when suddenly Emma started whispering. I thought for a moment that I'd activated the crystal without realising it. But no, her lips were moving.

She whispered very confidingly, "You haven't got an Uncle Raymond in Birmingham, have you?"

My mouth went dry. "Yes I have," I squeaked. "Well, sort of."

"Sort of." I could see her smiling at me.

I paused for a moment. "OK, he doesn't live in Birmingham."

"Where does he live?"

I grinned. "Inside my head."

She smiled too. "I can always tell when you're lying, you know."

Then Emma leaned forward suddenly. "You've made quite a few lucky guesses lately, haven't you? Ever since, in fact, you got that crystal."

Chapter Five

Telling My Secret

That gave me quite a shock, I can tell you. Without realising it, Emma had stumbled onto my secret. Of course, she was saying it as a kind of joke.

"So can the crystal see the future?" she asked.

"Maybe," I teased.

"There's something sort of magical about it, isn't there?"

"Very definitely." I was still messing about, but not completely. Ever since I'd found out how special my crystal was, I'd longed to share the secret with someone – with Emma.

It's a bit like someone giving you a football. Yeah, you can play with it on your own – do kick-ups and stuff – but only for so long. After a while, you've got to have someone to kick the ball to, haven't you?

That was exactly how I felt about my crystal. It was only half the fun with just me knowing about it. I'll admit I so wanted to impress Emma too. And a diver's watch looks pretty dull when compared with a mind-reading crystal, doesn't it?

Of course, I remembered too what Mrs Jameson had said – how I must always keep the secret to myself. But way up here with Emma, I felt suddenly reckless and daring.

"Do you really want to know how I found out about your dad?"

"I so do," she cried. The leaves were forming a pattern of shadows over her face. I could hardly see her. It made me feel as if I was talking to her in a dream.

"I've wanted to tell you for so long, Emma."

"Tell me what?" she yelled.

"Do you promise to keep what I tell you a secret?"

"I promise to throw you off this tree if you don't tell me right now," she laughed.

Then all in a rush I blurted out, "I knew what was worrying your dad because I used my crystal to read his mind."

A flash of amusement passed across Emma's face. "So you can read minds, can you?"

"Sure can – with the help of my crystal," I added.

"Even mine?"

I nodded.

Still grinning, she said, "Prove it."

"No problem. Think of a number and I'll tell you instantly what that number is."

Emma was still smiling away. "Right, I'm thinking of my number."

"Wait a sec. You've got to let my crystal warm up."

"Oh it has to warm up, does it? A bit like my gran's old telly!"

She was laughing again while I frowned with concentration. I'd never known the crystal feel so icy cold. It was absolutely freezing. And it wasn't warming up as quickly as it usually did – just as if the crystal was resisting me because … because it knew what I was doing was wrong. A shiver ran up my spine.

I actually stopped. But then I saw that diver's watch on Emma's hand again.

I snatched the crystal up once more. I held it so tightly this time and – finally – heat began to course through it.

"Keep thinking of your number," I urged.

"You're taking so long I've forgotten what it was." And into my head Emma whispered:

Why on earth is Matt doing this? He can be so funny sometimes.

"Think of your number," I urged.

The crystal picked up:

This is silly, but seven … my number's seven.

I stared across at her. "Your number's seven."

A small gasp escaped from her lips before she said, "I bet people always think of seven, don't they?"

"No."

"Then this has to be a trick. You can't really read minds with that crystal."

"Oh yes I can," I began.

Emma still wasn't convinced. The wind stirred, setting the branches rattling and shaking. It was almost as if the tree was warning me to stop now.

But I just couldn't do that.

"Think of a word, any word you like, a word that doesn't exist, if you like." I was speaking really quickly like an over-eager salesman. "Go on." I couldn't hold the crystal any tighter.

Emma gave an uneasy laugh, then half-closed her eyes. At once the word came through to me:

Spuckle.

"Spuckle," I grinned. "What kind of word is that?"

"I know." She smiled, but her smile quickly vanished into the darkness. "But how were you able to …" her voice fell away. "How exactly did you do that, Matt?"

I waved the crystal at her.

"No, tell me the truth, please."

And I overheard:

If this is some kind of joke, Matt's carrying it too far.

"It's not some kind of joke, Emma," I said.

She choked off a cry. Then all at once she started to scramble down the tree.

"Emma, where are you going?"

"Why don't you wave your crystal at me and find out," she cried. "No, I'll save you the trouble. I'm getting as far away from you as possible."

Chapter Six

The Crystal's Powers

I watched Emma with mounting horror. I couldn't let her go like this.

"Hey!" I started to clamber down after her. She was so worked up I was worried she might fall. But actually it was me who lost my footing.

Want to know the worst thing about crashing from a tree? You drop down backwards. You can't even try to do it in a cool way, or make out you meant to do it. For good measure, I landed with a mighty thump in a very large puddle.

And I didn't blame Emma for nearly killing herself laughing. I was just relieved she hadn't charged off.

She did then ask, "Are you all right, Matt?"

I scrambled to my feet, wiped my eyes – mud had spluttered everywhere – and then shook myself just the way dogs do when they've got wet. "Yeah, I'm absolutely fine. In fact, it's the only way to travel."

"You've got some sort of weed stuck in your hair – it suits you, actually." She giggled and I started to laugh too – until I realised that I had lost my crystal again. It must have slipped off my belt when I fell.

It was Emma who found it. It had rolled onto a pile of dead leaves.

"Here's your magic crystal," she said.

"Thanks." I carefully put it back on my belt.

She stood right in front of me. "So what am I thinking now?"

I tilted my crystal towards her, and moments later I overheard:

I thought my head would explode with shock when I realised Matt actually could read my mind. It was so weird – and scary

48

somehow!

I repeated word for word what she'd been thinking.

She stared at me. "I just can't believe it. You – my funny old Matt," (she said this with a wide smile), "being able to … it's just incredible."

I nodded, enjoying her wonderment.

"So, how long have you had the crystal?"

We climbed back up the tree and I told her the whole story. She listened, hardly saying anything, only exclaiming at certain events.

When I'd finished, she said, "And you haven't told anyone else about your crystal's power?"

"Only you."

"Only me!" She let out a pleased sigh. "And it will work on anyone?"

"Oh yes."

Her dark eyes glowed at me. "Prove it then."

We scrambled back down and made for the high street. There was hardly anyone about. The first person we saw – of all people – was Finn. He just nodded at us. He was sitting on a wall by himself on the opposite side of the road.

I let Emma borrow the crystal. She tapped into him. Afterwards, I asked her what Finn had been thinking.

She smiled. "First of all he wondered if we'd noticed his new trainers."

"How pathetic."

"Then he couldn't understand why I was going around with you, Spud, and not him. He was furious about it, actually … Bit sad really."

"Don't go feeling sorry for him," I cried accusingly.

"I'm not."

"The nerve of him thinking that," I muttered.

"Matt, he's free to think what he likes," laughed Emma.

Next we spotted a well-dressed man with thinning brown hair strolling in front of us. Again, I let Emma tune into him. He was imagining himself scoring the winning goal in a cup final. Emma kept whispering bits to me.

Then she rushed forward, tapped the man on the shoulder and said. "Brilliant goal."

The man let out a cry and jumped right up in the air, just as if a firework had exploded in his trousers.

"Did you see that?" exclaimed Emma. "Look at him."

The man was now half-running away from us. He kept turning back, gazing at us in fear and amazement.

"He can't believe his ears," cried Emma.

"And are you surprised?" I replied. "You've just read his most private, secret thoughts. Actually, we've got to be careful."

"I know, I know." She shook her head. "This crystal is so incredibly powerful, isn't it?"

We were silent for a moment, then we thought of that man leaping up into the air and we both started to laugh. Soon, tears were falling down our faces and still we couldn't stop.

After that, we climbed up the tree again. It was getting late. We should have both set off home now. But neither of us could stop talking about the crystal.

Then Emma said, "On Friday when you asked me who I liked … you used the crystal on me, didn't you?"

I hung my head a bit. "Afraid so."

"And you picked up that I thought you were fit." Immediately, a smile started to spread across my face. "But I was afraid if we went out together it would ruin our friendship."

"Yes," I said quietly.

"Yet tonight," she said. "You took a chance telling me about the crystal. I think I can take one too. So if you still want to go out with me …"

I could only nod. Happiness took all my words away.

We agreed we wouldn't tell anyone about us yet. People like Finn would only make stupid jokes all the time. We'd wait and pick the right moment.

"Will you promise me just one thing?" said Emma. "You won't ever use the crystal on me, because I have horrible thoughts sometimes that aren't true and well … I'd never have a private moment."

"I promise," I cried. "And if you ever find out I have used it on you, you can have the crystal."

I glanced down at the wood below. It was very dark and still. It was also full of shadows

… and then I saw one of those shadows start to move. It rose up out of the darkness and started darting among the trees.

My flesh froze. I thought at first it was Mrs Jameson, come to haunt me for breaking my promise and not keeping the secret.

I hissed to Emma, "Someone's down there."

"Listening to us?" Her voice was suddenly hushed.

"Could be." I suddenly realised that we'd both been talking about the crystal at the top of our voices. That person could be waiting down there ready to jump us and steal my crystal.

We squinted into the darkness, and then Emma cried out. "It's a cat."

Ghostly green eyes stared up at us, then slipped away. Emma let out a great sigh of relief. I didn't say anything, but I still had a few doubts. What if there had been someone else prowling about there as well as the cat? Someone creeping about in the darkness, taking in everything we'd said.

But after a few minutes, my doubts started to fade away. It had just been a cat, hadn't it? I noticed – yet again! – Finn's watch on Emma's wrist. And I said, "I wish I had a present to give you to remember tonight."

"Well, I'll tell you what," said Emma. "At my little cousin's tea party yesterday, I got this." She dug in her pocket and produced a gold-looking ring with a white sparkly stone. "I like it, so why don't you give me that?"

"A ring from a cracker?"

"It's the thought that counts." She handed me the ring. Then, feeling a bit silly, I gave the ring back to her. She placed it on her finger.

"One day soon I'll get you a much better one," I said.

"I'll keep this ring for ever," she replied.

The next morning should have been bright and sunny. In fact, it was drizzling, but it didn't matter at all. I was just so jubilant I'd told Emma about the crystal. And I was convinced that shadow I'd seen had only been a cat – until I reached my school.

There, stuck to my locker, was an envelope with my name in capitals on the outside. I ripped it open. Inside was a folded-up piece of paper torn from an exercise book. The words yelled out at me: I KNOW ABOUT THE CRYSTAL.

Chapter Seven

Blackmail

I immediately showed Emma the note.

She was horror-struck. "You were right, Matt. Someone was eavesdropping on us. Still," she added slowly, "at least we know it was someone from this school."

"And that someone was Finn," I said. "It's got to be him."

But Emma wasn't so sure.

"Come on, we saw him last night, didn't we? What do you bet he followed us?"

"Well, don't say anything to him yet," urged Emma. "We don't want to rattle him, otherwise, well, he could do anything."

For the rest of the day, I tailed Finn with my crystal. I didn't pick up anything incriminating at first. But then I overheard him thinking about the English test on *Julius Caesar* this Wednesday. He was worrying about it as the results would go on our report.

Then, after school, a second envelope was stuck to my locker. I tore it open feeling sick inside even before I'd read it. This one had been written on a computer. It said:

I will keep your secret about the crystal on one condition. You must tell me what questions will be in the English test on *Julius Caesar* on Wednesday. You can read Mrs Stacey's mind and find out. Then leave the questions in the empty locker (number sixty-six) on the bottom left hand side, straight after school tomorrow. Do not wait for me or try and see me.

If you fail to follow my instructions, I will tell every single person about your crystal. Obey them and I won't bother you again.

I showed the note to Emma. She looked really miserable. "This is all my fault. If you hadn't told me about the crystal, none of this would have happened."

"Now you're just being silly." I didn't blame Emma at all, but I did blame myself. And those nasty notes had certainly taken the shine off last night.

On the way home, we talked about what I should do.

I said, "If I find out the questions I'll be giving in to blackmail, and Finn will come back again and again, won't he?"

"But he said he wouldn't bother you any more."

"Do you believe that?"

Emma smiled faintly. "I want to."

I shook my head. "I could wait by the lockers after school and—"

"And er, what?"

"Fight him."

Emma started tut-tutting. "And what good will that do? He'll definitely go off and tell everyone about the crystal then."

Emma was right. I had no choice but to give in to blackmail this one time.

Next day in English, I scrutinised my class. I was pretty certain it was Finn who'd been writing to me. But I suppose everyone in the class was a suspect. I did a bit of surfing and picked up that a lot of other people in the class were worried about the *Julius Caesar* test tomorrow. But it didn't really get me any further.

At the end of the lesson, everyone rushed off for lunch while I hovered around. Emma whispered, "Good luck," then she left too.

The English teacher, Mrs Stacey, had taught at my school for years. She was a good teacher – helpful, but brisk and no-nonsense. However, for some reason, she liked me.

I moved towards her, clutching my crystal.

"Yes, Matt, what can I do for you?"

"I just wanted to ask you about the test tomorrow."

"What about it?"

"Well, I wondered if there'd be a question about the quarrel between Cassius and Brutus."

"Now, Matt, you know I can't tell you that.

But you'll be fine tomorrow." She turned her back on me. "Now off you go."

Mrs Stacey was busy thinking about a concert she'd be attending that night, and how she'd do all her preparation in her free period after lunch.

But I needed Mrs Stacey to be thinking about what was in the test – not her plans for tonight.

I uttered a kind of yelp.

She turned round, alarmed.

"What's wrong, Matt?"

"Nothing, Miss, I just feel a little bit faint. Is it all right if I sit down for a minute?" I gave another little yelp and fell onto a chair.

I had all her attention now. She was leaning over me. I could smell her breath. It reeked of coffee. "Matt, do you want me to get the nurse?"

"No, no," I said hastily. "It's just I've been up late revising *Julius Caesar.*"

She looked concerned. "But, Matt, you're a good student. You needn't worry."

"I do, though. I've been worrying for hours, wondering if there'll be a question on omens and superstitions, or the battles at the end of the play …"

She pulled up a chair. She began to talk about *Julius Caesar* and, more importantly, to think about it. The crystal picked up four of the six questions in tomorrow's test (and we only had to answer three). As I heard the questions, I realised that I was cheating too. I'd know what was going to be in the test as well.

After I left Mrs Stacey, I ran off to the back field and wrote the questions down. At the bottom I added: *I will not do this for you ever again.*

Then, at the end of school, I made for locker sixty-six. It was dented right in the middle and the lock was permanently broken. Inside was a pair of old, stinky football boots. They smelt as if they'd been in there since the school was built.

I took them out and cleared the locker of all its antique sweet papers. Then I folded up the question sheet and slipped it inside.

Only Emma knew what I was doing. She gave my hand a squeeze. We walked out of school together.

"I've got to know who's sending me these

notes," I said.

"But he – or she – said not to wait," cried Emma.

"I won't wait by the school," I said. "But I'll keep watch."

Our school was at the end of a road. Along the road was a bakery and coffee shop. Emma and I could stake out in there, and then we'd see anyone returning to school.

"We must be very clever," said Emma. "If we do see Finn or someone else from our class, we've got to follow them, but they mustn't know we're on to them."

At that very moment, Finn passed the window. He was on his way back to school all right. We both ducked down.

"Did he see us?" asked Emma.

"I don't think so."

"Look, I'm going to trail him," I said.

"I think it's best I go after him," said Emma. "I won't get as worked up as you." She got up. "You wait here. I won't be long."

I ordered another coffee. But I couldn't drink it. My insides were turning somersaults.

And then I saw two more girls from my English class half-running towards the school.

I had a sudden, horrible thought. What if more than one person knew about the crystal? Maybe both those girls had written the note.

I had to follow them.

Chapter Eight

My Superpower

The two girls walked quickly into school.

I followed at what I hoped was a safe distance. Finn was still my chief suspect, but anyone from my English group could have written that note.

The two girls were making for the cloakroom. They walked over to the lockers. My heart was pumping away now.

"Here it is!" cried one of the girls. She fished out a copy of *Julius Caesar*.

"So relieved I haven't lost it!" she exclaimed. "I knew I'd put it somewhere safe – just couldn't remember where."

The two girls went off giggling and chatting together.

A hand touched me on the shoulder. I sprang round.

"I thought I told you to stay in the café?" It was Emma.

"Did Finn take the questions?" I asked.

"I'm not sure," said Emma. "He went past the lockers all right but by the time I got near him, he was rushing off to the science block. I followed him and spotted him talking to one of the teachers about something. Then he went out of school again."

We piled over to locker sixty-six.

"We'll soon know what Finn's been up to," I announced.

I opened it up. Then I turned to Emma. "The questions have vanished."

Emma paled. "I'm sorry, Matt. I didn't want Finn to spot me so I kept way back."

"Don't you worry, we've got all the evidence we need. It's him all right."

"We don't know for certain he——"

"I do and I'll soon catch him up."

I just assumed Emma would come with me. Instead she said, "Let me know what happens … and don't … well, be careful, won't you?"

I sped off, half-running, and soon caught sight of Finn slouching along. I yelled out to him to stop. He must have heard me, but instead he ducked into Mr and Mrs Kossoff's sweet shop.

I spotted him at once – pretending to study the games at the back of the shop. Otherwise, the shop was empty – except for Spider-Man.

Well, actually, a tall guy in a blue and red Spider-Man costume. He was strutting round the shop and casually flinging anything that caught his fancy straight into his own bag. You'd have thought he was a very confident burglar if Mr and Mrs Kossoff weren't standing together behind the counter silently watching him.

Mr Kossoff was staring straight ahead, his face deathly white. Mrs Kossoff looked equally tense but was bright red.

"What's going on?" I hissed.

"Nothing at all," murmured Mrs Kossoff and Mr Kossoff gave me the most unconvincing smile you've ever seen.

I hastily directed my crystal at them. I've never known it work so fast, and within seconds I picked up from Mr Kossoff:

At first he only wanted a few things from us but now he's become so greedy, and is taking so much I don't know what to do. I just wish I felt stronger. Ten years ago I'd have seen him off, even five ...

I was hot with anger. And I knew I had to help the Kossoffs. That's why I said to Spider-Man, "Hey you, stop!" Only my voice wasn't working properly and even I didn't hear me. So I tried again and this time switched the volume up so loudly that my words rocketed around the shop. "Hey you, stop, put the bag down and go!"

"Matt, please don't get involved," cried Mrs Kossoff at once.

"Everything is absolutely fine," added Mr Kossoff.

Then Spider-Man spun round. "I'd do what they say and mind your own business." He had a strong American accent.

"Well, I'm making it my business." Someone had said that in a film once. And now, incredibly, I was saying it. No wonder this moment seemed as dream-like as when I told Emma about the crystal.

Mr and Mrs Kossoff's mouths were opening and closing like stunned goldfish. They couldn't believe what I was doing. Neither could I!

Spider-Man glided towards me. He had a springy, bouncy walk. He loomed over me. "Come on then," he laughed and started jabbing the air with his fists.

Mrs Kossoff let out a stricken cry. "Matt, love, please don't get involved ..." she began.

"It's all right." I said this so calmly and confidently I even convinced myself for a moment that I knew what I was doing. The shop fell utterly silent, save for Finn at the back of the shop crunching a sweet, just as if he were watching all this at the cinema.

I clenched one hand into a fist. I couldn't remember the last time I was in a fight. I just knew I was rubbish at it. And for a few petrified seconds I wondered how I could have been so stupid. I wasn't going to help the Kossoffs, only humiliate myself in front of them – not to mention Finn.

But I was forgetting something absolutely vital. I have a super power. No one else I knew had one. Only me. Time to summon it.

I lowered my head, clutching the crystal and concentrating fiercely. Very soon I heard from Spider-Man:

Come on, stay cool, Rupert. You can see off this joker in seconds and those old codgers will be more in my power than ever. One punch will be enough for this clown.

But warned when he was about to swing at me, I was able to dodge – rather superbly – his punch. This shocked him so much, his legs actually buckled backwards and Spider-Man nearly fell over.

The Kossoffs cheered me as if I'd actually sent him flying. This gave me confidence and as he advanced towards me again, I yelled, "You're not fit to wear Spider-Man's costume! You're a disgrace, Rupert!"

He just called me Rupert. But he doesn't know me. So how could he know my name? It's not possible.

All at once he sounded so panicky, so freaked out, that I saw with a start that I'd done it. Or my crystal had.

I'D UNCOVERED HIS WEAKNESS.

So I roared, "Yes, I know all about you. Just wait until I tell your parents what mean, cruel things you've been doing, Rupert."

Do you know, he actually reeled back from me then, as if I'd punched him dead hard. "You go near my house and you'll be very, very sorry!" he snarled.

But his voice was shaking and that phoney American accent had completely vanished.

"Rupert, if you don't exit now I'll ..."

But I was addressing an empty space.

Spider-Man had vanished – and without his bag of booty.

Mrs Kossoff took a deep breath, and then another one, while Mr Kossoff wiped his forehead and said, "He's gone … he's actually gone. I can't believe it."

"He's been threatening you for a while, hasn't he?" I said.

"From almost the very first day we got back," said Mrs Kossoff. "He just burst into our shop in that costume, demanding free things and then throwing our stuff about when we refused."

"I allowed him to intimidate us," interrupted Mr Kossoff. He shook his head very angrily. "I've been very weak."

"But you haven't been at all well," murmured Mrs Kossoff.

"And he took you by surprise," I said.

"Yes, that's it," agreed Mr Kossoff. "But you dared to stand up to him and showed him up for what he really is – a coward."

Even Finn, who'd been watching all this intently muttered, "Yeah, you did all right." Although outside the shop, Finn had to add, "But you were so lucky knowing that guy's name. How did you? I've not seen him before."

"Never mind all that," I said briskly. "You've been sending me stupid notes, haven't you?"

For a few seconds, Finn's eyes darted about like a cornered animal. Then he laughed a bit too loudly. "Well, I heard you up in that tree, boasting to Emma about how you had a crystal that could read minds."

I felt myself going super tense. Finn laughed again. "You were so jealous of the present I gave Emma, weren't you?"

"No," I began.

"Don't lie, Spud. That's why you made up that far-fetched rubbish about your crystal – to try and out-class me. And Emma was actually starting to believe it ..." – he sniggered – "until I challenged you to read Mrs Stacey's mind. Of course, I knew there wouldn't be any test questions in that locker."

He sounded so pleased with himself I could only gape at him. But they were there. And he'd snatched them, hadn't he?

"I'm just amazed Emma even fell for it," he scoffed. "But she knows the truth about your stupid crystal now all right, doesn't she?"

Was this all a massive bluff on Finn's part?

Or had someone else grabbed the questions?

Later, me and my crystal would find out. But I'd had more than enough of Finn for one day. So instead I shot off to Emma's house. I had so much to tell her.

And yet, as I related to her my latest adventures, Emma seemed distracted, as if she was thinking about something else. I ended by saying, "So what do you think? Did Finn take the questions or not?"

For the first time since I'd arrived, Emma looked right at me. "You and your crystal will uncover the truth." Before I could reply she went on, "But you know already, don't you?"

"No I don't. How could I?"

She gave a horrible laugh. "Be honest, Matt."

"I am and I don't know what you're talking about ..." I began, but then I stopped.

And in that instant, I did know.

Chapter Nine

Message from Mrs Jameson

The shock flooded my head.

"It was you," I stuttered.

"Yes," whispered Emma. Then she burst out, "I didn't mean to. But when you know your parents are desperate for you to get good grades, and you're about to disappoint them yet again … and there are the actual questions … One quick peek, that's all I intended until I heard someone coming. So I had to take them with me. But as soon as I got home I tore them up into tiny little pieces. I'm sure Mum thought I'd gone mad. But it's too late, isn't it? I'm a cheat."

"Well, sort of, but …"

"I'm a cheat," she repeated. "I'm also a double-agent."

"What …?" I began.

"Well, I let you go chasing after Finn when I knew he didn't have the questions."

"He still wrote those horrible notes."

"That doesn't matter," she said.

"Of course it does. Look, Emma—"

"No, don't start being nice to me. I let myself down – and I know it. There was a distinctly strained silence for a moment and then Emma said, "I'm relieved you know – even though you broke your promise to me."

I stared at her, thoroughly confused.

"Don't look like that. You've used the crystal on me, haven't you?"

"No!" I was indignant.

"Matt, it's fine."

"But I haven't …"

She sighed loudly and disbelievingly. "So how did you know I took the questions then?"

"Well, I …"

"Go on." Her voice rose.

"I just suddenly sensed it, and I know that sounds a bit lame."

"A bit!" she exclaimed.

"OK, I just looked at you and had this very bad feeling."

Emma gave a mocking laugh.

"No, what I meant to say—"

"It's all right," interrupted Emma. "We've both messed up today."

But I hadn't. Why wouldn't Emma believe me?

Then she jumped up. "Do me a favour."

"Just name it."

"Go home."

"What! Now?"

"Yeah, right now," she said.

"OK, but …"

"I'd really like to be on my own for a bit, Matt."

I'd thought telling Emma about the crystal would bring us closer together but instead …

"See you tomorrow then," I said, as cheerfully as I could.

I skulked home and immediately my mum

started fussing about and being incredibly nice to me. She hadn't been like this since I had mumps over two years ago.

Something odd was going on here. So I used my crystal on Mum and eventually discovered that Mrs Stacey had rung and told Mum she thought I was overworking.

I also picked up that Mum was changing her mind about getting me a dog. She decided I needed something to take my attention off my schoolwork. Normally, I'd have been over the moon. But everything felt ruined now.

Next morning, I looked forward to seeing Emma – yet I was nervous too. I decided to talk about Spurs – anything except what had happened yesterday.

But she didn't go to school. She was too ill, her mum said. So after all that fuss, she missed the *Julius Caesar* test.

I only attempted the two questions I hadn't 'overheard'. Every time I stopped and looked up, Mrs Stacey was smiling encouragingly at me. I felt such a fraud.

Then after school, I thought of Emma. What

a mess it all was.

I suddenly wondered if Mrs Jameson had ever tried to share the crystal's secret with anyone. I bet she had. And what would she advise me to do now? I so wished I knew. I even found myself standing outside her house. There was a FOR SALE sign outside it, and the garden, which she'd looked after so carefully, was thick with weeds.

I didn't know what I was doing here. Mrs Jameson wasn't suddenly going to pop up and help me. Not even my crystal could conjure up Mrs Jameson again.

But I still held it in my hand and thought, "Mrs Jameson, I can't believe you're far away from your beloved crystal. Maybe I shouldn't have told Emma about it, but I have done. What should I do now? Help me, somehow, please."

Then I went into the local shop just across the road from Mrs Jameson's house. I'd been in there many times before on errands for her, and the old shopkeeper recognised me. We chatted for a bit.

I still had the crystal in my hand. Without

me realising it, the crystal was squeezing itself out of my hand. All at once, it fell from my grasp and on to a stack of newspapers, tied up with string, on the ground beside me.

I knelt down. It was our local paper. The crystal had landed on the bottom of the page. I picked it up. Underneath the crystal was a small photograph of a woman and a caption:

LOTTERY WIN COST ME ALL MY FRIENDS
Full story page seven

Without knowing why, I persuaded the shopkeeper to untie the papers so I could buy one. I walked home reading page seven.

So this woman called Lily had won three million on the lottery. Lily said the news had changed her friends' attitude to her immediately. Their first thought was, "What's in it for me?" They all came to her with a shopping list of things they wanted.

Lily was indignant and hurt and felt her friends were just using her. She fell out with them all. But then she said, "I realised something as amazing as a lottery win was bound to set my friends dreaming. Now I want them to contact me."

At home, I read the article again and again. I kept thinking of Emma. If a lottery win set friends dreaming, so would a crystal that could read minds. Actually, my crystal was far more amazing than any lottery win.

Fancy just blurting out that I had a superpower. I'd told Emma far too quickly, hadn't I? No wonder her head was turned and she did something so out of character. And now she felt an aching disappointment with herself about it. But she shouldn't feel guilty – I should!

I remembered suddenly how the crystal had seemed to just slip out of my hand and land right on top of that particular newspaper, that particular caption. Had Mrs Jameson meant me to see it? Was that her way of advising me?

For a moment, I forgot to breathe – I was so excited. I was certain it wasn't just a coincidence. I was certain of something else too. It was up to me to sort things out with Emma right now.

Chapter Ten

The Only Way

I whizzed round to Emma's house straight after tea. I still wasn't sure exactly what I was going to say to her. Or what reaction I'd get.

Her mum answered the door. "Oh, hello, Matt," she said. I stepped inside the narrow hallway. Normally, she'd have told me to go right upstairs. Today, she just gave me this highly embarrassed smile.

"How's Emma?" I asked.

"She's had a terrible migraine all day."

"Could I see her?"

Emma's mum looked even more embarrassed.

"Actually, Matt, she said if you called she didn't want to see you today."

"Oh, OK." My voice fell away.

"Have you two had a falling out?"

"Sort of."

"Well, I wouldn't worry too much. I think she's very stressed at the moment." She lowered her voice. "Last night I caught her tearing this piece of paper up into smaller and smaller pieces. Now why would she do that?"

Because they were the 'stolen' test questions on *Julius Caesar*, that's why. But I didn't say this, of course.

"Now, her father and I want her to do well at school, but not at the expense of her health. Above all, we want her to be happy."

The phone rang.

"Oh, will you excuse me, Matt?"

She rushed away. I hesitated for just a second, and then sprinted upstairs. Emma and I shouldn't be hiding from each other. And we had to clear the air right now.

I knocked on her door. No answer. So I opened the door very slowly.

"Hi Emma, it's me. How are you doing?"

Still no answer.

Then I saw why. Emma was fast asleep. I was about to creep out again, when I remembered something.

With the aid of my crystal, I can talk to people when they're asleep. They hear me, and I can overhear their thoughts.

I held the crystal and after it had warmed up, said, "Emma, can you hear me?"

"Yes, I can." Her voice sounded heavy with sleep. "But how? Is this a dream?"

"Yes, Emma, you could say that."

"Well, I want you to go away."

I was hurt. "You don't mean that."

"Oh yes I do," she hissed.

"Look, Emma, listen," I began.

"No, you listen. I'm very ashamed about what I did yesterday."

"Don't be. Anyway, it was much more my fault. I told you about the crystal."

"The crystal," Emma repeated. "I still can't believe what it can do. It's really unsettled me. I so wish you hadn't told me about it."

By now, the crystal was scorching hot so I had to let go of it. But Emma's last words tore round my head. *"I so wish you hadn't told me about it."*

Suddenly I knew what I had to do next.

Once, when my sister, Alison, was asleep, I'd used the crystal to sort of hypnotise her. It was the only way to get her to forget about the crystal's powers. It had been for the best. Now I had to try and do the same to Emma.

I picked up the crystal. It had cooled down enough. I said, "Emma, it's me again."

She groaned.

"I'm going to help you. Just repeat after me—"

Suddenly I heard footsteps on the stairs. I had to act fast.

"Repeat after me. Sunday night never happened. It's gone from my memory."

"Sunday night never happened. It's gone from my memory," she chanted.

"And the crystal—" But I couldn't say any more because Emma's mum was in the doorway, staring at me in bewilderment.

"Matthew, I thought I told you—"

"I know, I'm sorry, but I was sure I could talk her round – only she's asleep."

That's when Emma muttered, "And the crystal."

Emma's mum leant forward. "What's that, love?"

"And the crystal," she muttered again.

Emma's mum just shook her head. "Poor girl, she's got herself so worked up, she's not making sense. I think it's best you leave now, Matthew."

"Yeah, sure. Sorry."

I sped down those stairs. If only I'd been able to have a few moments longer with Emma.

Now I didn't know if I'd wiped the crystal from Emma's mind or not.

Chapter Eleven

A Terrible Shock

The next day Emma was still away from school. I planned to go and see her again later. But when I got home, my mum was waiting for me, smiling. She'd arranged for me to choose a dog from the Animal Rescue Centre.

Dad was still away, but Alison came with Mum and me. The dog was to be my responsibility. I could pick the one I wanted, only not a big dog.

The dogs were in pens and as soon as they saw us they started barking madly.

"How do you stand the noise?" Mum asked the assistant who was showing us round.

"What noise?" replied the assistant.

As we walked by the dogs, they ran to the front of their pens, showing themselves off. All except one, a brown and white spaniel. He just hid in the corner.

The assistant pointed at the spaniel. "Poor Scampi. He was in such a bad way when he came in here, all his hair had gone."

"Oh, that's terrible," I cried.

"And he'd been so badly neglected, he had to go on a special diet because his stomach had shrunk."

No wonder the dog looked so miserable.

"He's very affectionate to us," said the assistant, "but he's still very shy, so he keeps getting overlooked."

"I think he might take quite a bit of looking after," said Mum, half-pulling me away. She was pointing at a terrier that was jumping about and wagging his tail furiously. "Now, he looks ideal," she said.

But my eyes kept going back to Scampi.

Suddenly I grabbed the crystal. I can't pick up a dog's thoughts from it but dogs can pick up mine. I tilted it towards Scampi and thought:

*Scampi, you're a good dog, aren't you?
And do you want to come back with me?*

Scampi's ears pricked up. I knew he could hear me so I carried on:

Scampi, if you want to come away with me, go over to the front of the pen now. Come on, boy, hurry up.

The next moment, Scampi was pressing his nose right through the front of the pen. I went over to him. He looked up at me, and then licked one of my fingers.

I knew he was the dog I had to have. Mum sighed a lot but agreed. We had a special chat with the assistant, who said she would visit us soon to see how Scampi was settling down.

Scampi slept on my lap all the way home. "He seems to have taken to you, anyway," said Mum.

When we got home, Mum let Scampi have

a wander around downstairs. Then he just ran round and round the garden as if he couldn't believe his luck – he was somewhere decent at last.

Mum gave me a long lecture on how I was taking on special responsibilities with Scampi. He still had an infection in his eyes and needed eye drops twice a day. It was up to me to remember, not Mum. She also said how Scampi was never to be allowed upstairs.

"Couldn't he just put two paws in my bedroom?" I asked.

"If I see him upstairs, he goes back right away," said Mum. She made up a basket for Scampi downstairs and said if he cried in the night, on no account was I to go to him, otherwise we'd never get any peace.

I wasn't asleep long when his whining woke me up. I crept out on to the landing. A floorboard creaked and Mum called out, "No, Matt, I told you, leave him."

But it was hard to leave him, especially as he sounded so unhappy.

Then I decided to try something. I stole out

on to the landing again, held my crystal tightly and thought:

Scampi, can you hear me, can you?

Scampi gave a kind of yelp in reply.

Good boy, now listen. Don't cry, you're in your new home – and everything's going to be great now.

I went on like this for ages. Scampi's cries gradually became fainter, and then they stopped altogether.

Next morning my mum congratulated me. "Well done, Matt, for not going downstairs to Scampi. I told you he'd soon settle down, didn't I?"

I smiled to myself.

The doorbell rang. To my great surprise it was Emma.

"Well, don't look so shocked. I've only been away a couple of days," said Emma.

Then Scampi appeared behind my legs. Of

course, Emma loved Scampi instantly, and we were both playing with him until Mum shooed us off to school.

We walked along together, chatting about Scampi. Emma seemed her old self again. So had my plan worked? Had she forgotten all about the crystal?

"One good thing about being away," she said, "I missed the *Julius Caesar* test. Were the questions hard?"

I stopped dead. "Yeah, a real Mrs Stacey special. I could only do two of them."

"I bet I couldn't have done any of them. I always seem to revise the wrong things. Still, last night I had this long chat with my mum and dad, and they said as long as I try, that's all they ask. They were really nice about it, actually."

So far, so good. I was tempted to use my crystal just to check Emma had really forgotten all about its powers. But in the end I didn't.

Then, with a jolt, I noticed something. Emma wasn't wearing the ring I'd given her to mark us going out together.

"Where's your ring gone?" I asked.

She grinned. "I was laughing about that ring with my mum this morning. I can't imagine why I've had that on my finger for the past few days. Mum thinks it's because I was over-stressed."

I stopped dead. "But I gave you that ring."

"Oh, very funny. I remember where it came from all right – out of a cracker at my cousin's party."

"But you gave me the ring to give to you because …"

She leant across and felt my forehead. "Matt, what are you gabbling about? That ring is nothing to do with you. How could it be?"

She was smiling, but looked puzzled as well.

With mounting horror, I realised what I'd done. I'd removed the crystal from her memory all right, but I'd wiped out everything else from that evening too – including us going out together.

I walked around school in a daze all day. How could I have made Emma forget something so important as us going out together? I'd just have to ask her out again.

After school, Emma came back to my

house. Mum had stocked up with doggy things, including a collar and lead for Scampi. We took Scampi for a walk, and then introduced him to Emma's dog, Bess. She sniffed this new impostor suspiciously at first, but soon the two dogs were tearing around the garden together.

And there were celebrations at Emma's house too. Her dad had just rung through to say he hadn't been selected for redundancy. Emma's mum admitted she'd been going out of her mind waiting.

Then she took me aside and whispered, "I'm really pleased you and Emma have sorted yourselves out."

But we hadn't sorted ourselves out. That was the problem.

So later, when Emma and I were sitting in the garden watching the two dogs playing together, I asked her out again.

She turned me down flat. "I've been so dreading you asking me that. I do like you, Matt. Of course I do. But if we went out together, and it didn't work out … well, we'd have nothing. And I'd have lost my very best mate. So I don't think I could ever take that chance."

I wanted to say to her, "But you did take that chance – and only a few nights ago." But, of course, she didn't remember anything about that now. That moment was lost forever.

"I'm so sorry, Matt."

I shrugged awkwardly. "Don't worry about it."

Maybe Emma had only agreed to go out with me on Sunday because I had a magic crystal.

I'd never know now.

That was the problem with the crystal. It mixed up everything, including me – especially me!

I was supposed to stay at Emma's for my tea. Instead, I faked a stomach ache and said I'd go home. But actually I took Scampi for another walk. The air was so frosty it stung my eyes. I walked on, going much further than I'd intended, right on to the outskirts of the town. Scampi was enjoying himself anyway, sniffing everything appreciatively.

I felt so fed up, I took the crystal off my belt. I stared into it, watching all the different colours twisting and curling like a nest of snakes.

"What do I want to hear people's thoughts for anyway?" I muttered. "It's such a stupid thing to do."

And that's when a high-pitched voice whispered right in my ear:

What am I going to do? Someone help me, please!

Chapter Twelve

Merlin to the Rescue

It was as if my crystal had just received a distress signal. And I couldn't ignore it, especially as the voice had sounded so young.

The crystal was pointing towards a back street I'd never noticed before. "Come on, Scampi," I said. "We'll have a quick look, then we'll go home."

A second-hand bookshop took up the whole street. Sprawled down one side were ancient armchairs, sofas, and cabinets. Opposite, in front of a huge garage, loomed a small army of clapped-out fridges and cookers.

A man lurked in the shop doorway. He was a large, sweaty-looking man with tiny, suspicious eyes. Scampi gave a growl.

"Tie your dog up before you come in here."

"Shan't bother," I replied.

It certainly wasn't him the crystal had overheard. Scampi and I wandered on down the street. The man stood watching us for a bit, then he went back inside his shop.

No one else seemed to be about. Yet the crystal had definitely overheard someone. I held it in front of me as if it were a metal detector searching out buried treasure.

The crystal quickly found that voice again. This is what I overheard:

Mum said, get out of my sight, William. I never want to see you again. And she won't. But what am I going to do? I can't stay here.

Yet the voice still seemed to be coming out of thin air.

We were at the end of the street now. All that

faced us was a large brown wardrobe. Scampi gave another growl. "Do you hear someone too?" I whispered.

With a yank, I opened the wardrobe door. And there, shrinking at the back, was a small boy who couldn't have been more than five or six.

I stared at him.

He stared back at me.

"Any particular reason why you're hiding in that wardrobe?" I asked.

"Just leave me alone," hissed the boy.

"What's your name?" I asked.

"Can't tell you that."

"It wouldn't be William, would it?"

The boy jumped in amazement. "But how did you know that?"

"Oh, I know lots of things – like you've run away from home, haven't you?"

"Yes," squeaked the boy, and then he added, "You're magic, aren't you?"

I grinned. "Just call me Merlin."

But the boy took me seriously. "You're not Merlin the magician, are you?"

"That's right, only I'm in disguise, so don't tell anyone."

"I won't," gasped the boy.

"Now, I command you to climb out of that wardrobe."

The boy obeyed instantly. He was shaking a bit. I think he was worried I was about to turn him into a toad.

"Why don't you give Scampi a pat?" I said.

The boy knelt down and gently, cautiously, patted Scampi.

"Tell me, what are you doing here?" I asked the boy.

"Don't you know?" he demanded.

"Of course I do. But I want you to tell me."

"All right, Merlin. Well, you know I broke my mum's favourite vase? And I really didn't mean to do it, but now she hates me. She said I'm nothing but trouble and she's sick of me. She told me to get out of her sight. And so I did."

"She thinks I'm in my room, but I crept out of the house and this bus pulled up, and I got on it. I sat with this woman and two other boys. They asked for a half-fare to Jericho Road, and so did

I. I used up all my money too."

"I got off with them, but they weren't very friendly. Then the woman said she was going to take me to the police station, but I ran and ran and now I've got to hide here … forever."

"You can't do that, William. You'll have to go back," I said.

"No, never," he cried.

"But I'm commanding you," I said.

"Oh." He looked up. "Will you magic us back?"

"No, we'll get the bus this time," I said. "I only use magic for special occasions these days."

The three of us caught the bus back to William's home in Clately. It was nearly seven miles away, and the fare used up all the money I had saved for Emma's birthday. William sat cuddling Scampi. He noticed my crystal and wanted to hold it.

"Maybe, later," I said.

Then the bus drew into William's road. Suddenly, he pointed at a woman who was talking animatedly into a mobile phone.

"That's my mum," he cried, "and she's going

to be so mad at me."

"No she won't," I said.

"Yes she will. She looks really angry." The bus jolted to a stop. William hissed, "I'm sorry, Merlin, but I can't get off this bus. Not even if you command me."

I thought quickly. "All right, William, I'm going to put a spell on you."

"Oooh." William looked both scared and excited.

"Here, hold my crystal."

He took the crystal.

Then I muttered (hoping no one else could hear me), "Hocus mucus, Merlin's magic spell will dawn. When this crystal starts to warm."

"Hocus mucus," I repeated for good measure.

William stared at me, transfixed. "Will those words work for anyone?"

"No, only me."

Then he exclaimed, "It's getting hot, Merlin!"

"Of course it is, my spell is working. Move the crystal towards the window and your mum."

"I don't want her to see me," said William, crouching down.

"My magic spell is this: Hocus mucus, whatever your mum thinks will pour into your ear."

William looked right at me, and then let out a cry. "It's my mum talking right in my ear like you said. Can she hear me?"

I shook my head.

"And she's saying, 'If anything's happened to William, I'll never forgive myself. Never. All that fuss over a stupid vase.' Now she's saying—"

The bus started to lurch forward. William looked at me, and then screeched. "Make the bus stop, Merlin."

"Only you can do that," I said.

So William let out a great yell of "Stop!" and the three of us scrambled off, just in time.

William's mum spotted her son and came flying towards us at a speed any Olympic athlete would have envied. She and William hugged and kissed each other while Scampi and I felt a bit awkward.

But William's mum insisted Scampi and I come inside for tea and cakes. We also met just about every one of the neighbours who'd all been out looking for William.

Then William's dad arrived – he'd rushed home from work. And later he insisted on driving me home (just as well, actually – I only had ten pence left) and telling my startled mum just what I'd done.

After he'd left, Mum said, "I'm really proud of you. If you hadn't discovered that boy, goodness knows what would have happened to him." Then she added, "But why did William's dad keep calling you Merlin?"

"Just a little nickname they gave me," I said.

Later that evening, I slipped off to the Kossoffs. I'd checked on them every morning and most evenings too.

And once again, there hadn't been a return performance from the fake Spider-Man. So instead I asked about them retiring.

"Did we really say that?" grinned Mr Kossoff.

"Well, we're not going anywhere. Not after seeing you stand up to ... that impostor," chipped in Mrs Kossoff.

She put out her hand and squeezed mine. "He

might have dressed up as a superhero but you acted like one."

"Superhero is, in fact, my middle name," I grinned.

So, in only the past few hours, I've been called Merlin the Magician and compared to a superhero. I'll be honest, I love having all these extra identities.

But I know it's all thanks to my crystal. And one day, when I'm very old and have to decide who to pass my crystal on to next, I'll write down everything I've learnt. A guide book from the crystal master!

I've already made a rule never to use it on family and friends. Now I'm adding, don't use it on the girl you'd like to be your girlfriend, either!

So far, I've kept to that promise. Well, almost. I am just using the crystal on one special friend. Guess who?

Every afternoon after I leave Emma, I pick up my crystal and start beaming thoughts to Scampi. His hearing, by the way, is amazing. He can pick up from over a mile away. I say to him, "Come on, Scampi, come and meet me. Go to the door, there's a good boy."

At once he starts scratching at the front door, whining to be let out. Then he charges off and sits right outside the gate just as I'm about to turn into my road.

My neighbours think it's uncanny how he always knows exactly when I'm coming home. So, if I'm late because of football practice, Scampi will just ask to be let out later too.

He never ever gets it wrong.

Half of my road comes out to observe this amazing phenomenon now. "It's magic to watch," one of them said yesterday.

Thanks to the crystal, my life is full of magic. And who knows, maybe one day I'll even pick up your thoughts. Wouldn't that be amazing?

I'll be listening.

About Pete Johnson

Pete's favourite subjects at school were English and history. His least favourite was maths.

He has always loved reading. When he was younger, Pete would read up to six books a week – even more in the school holidays!

His most favourite book as a child was *One Hundred and One Dalmatians*. He wrote to the author, Dodie Smith, and she encouraged him to become a writer.

Other childhood favourites include *The Witches* by Roald Dahl, *Tom's Midnight Garden* by Philippa Pearce and Enid Blyton's *The Mystery of the Invisible Thief*.

When he was younger, Pete used to sleepwalk. One night, he woke up in his pyjamas walking along a busy road.

He has a West Highland terrier called Hattie.

His favourite food is chocolate. He especially loves Easter eggs!

Pete loved to watch old black-and-white movies with his dad on Saturday night and used to review films on Radio 1. Sometimes he watched three films in a day! Pete has met lots of famous actors and collects signed film pictures.

He likes to start writing by eight o'clock in the morning. He reads all his books out loud to see if the dialogue sounds right. And if he's stuck for an idea, he goes for a long walk.

Wherever he goes, Pete always carries a notebook with him. "The best ideas come when you're least expecting them," he says. Why don't you try that too? Maybe you'll have a brilliant idea for your own book!

To find out more about Pete and his books, go to:

www.petejohnsonauthor.com

A Note from Pete

I really enjoy visiting book clubs. It is always exciting – and I'll be honest, a little scary – when you are discussing one of my books. Readers can – and do – say whatever they want!

Maybe you might want to start your own book club. So to get you going, here are a few suggestions. Of course you don't have to be in a book club – you can do it just for fun!

"I have a strange, eerie SUPERPOWER."
- What did you think when you first read those words?
- Do you think Matt's superpower is eerie – or even a bit spooky? Or is it exciting and fun? Give your reasons.
- Put cards marked with different superpowers in a bowl. Then pick a card and ask other

members of the book club to ask you questions about your life. See how long you can keep on pretending you have a superpower.

"The Whispering Ghosts chapter is so hilarious."
- That is what one reader wrote. Do you agree?
- Look at all the funny moments in this chapter. There are Finn's reactions, of course. But also the banter between Cameron and Matt. Look at the thoughts Matt sends to Finn ("So beware … Beware …!"). How seriously are we meant to take this?
- Did you feel sorry for Finn? Or do you think he deserves everything he gets?

Matt helps the Kossoffs
- We have watched Matt playing a trick on Finn, but here we see a different side to his character. What is the first thing he does to help the Kossoffs? (Look at Chapter Three.)
- Then he offers to help The Kossoffs again in Chapter Four. Why do you think they smile? What does Matt's offer tell you about him? What would you have done here?

Matt Superhero?
- In Chapter Eight, we see Matt at his bravest. What makes Matt hot with anger? Would you have felt the same?
- When Matt describes the moment he stands up to Spider-Man as "dream-like", what do you think he means?
- Matt is worried he is not going to help the Kossoffs, only "humiliate" himself in front of them. What saves him?
- Later, the Kossoffs say Matt acted like a superhero. What's your opinion?

Adults being bullied
- In this story we see two elderly people being picked on — and bullied. Did this surprise you? "I allowed him to intimidate us," said Mr Kossoff. "I've been very weak." Do you agree? Or do you understand why the Kossoffs gave in to the bully?
- The Kossoffs say Matt showed the bully up for what he really is. What do you think they meant?

Matt reveals his secret

- Why do you think Matt tells Emma about the crystal's power. Is it because he longed to share his secret with someone? Or that he wanted to impress Emma — and put Finn's birthday present in the shade? Or is there another reason?

- Is it fair to Emma to blurt out his secret like that? How would you have reacted on being told such an amazing secret. Have you ever kept a big secret from family and friends?

What kind of book is MindReader: Superhero?

- How would you describe it? A fantasy about having a magic power? Is it also a comedy? a school story? A mystery? A tale of friendship?

- Do you like the fact that this book is not confined to one genre?

- How would you compare it to the Louis the Laugh stories?

- Is Matt anything like Louis?

- Could you compare Emma to Maddy?

- Or Finn to Edgar?

- What was your favourite scene in the book?

Read all the MindReader adventures!

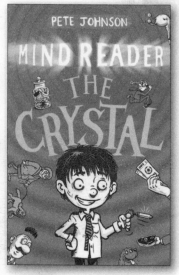

978-1-78270-303-7

978-1-78270-305-1

Also by Pete Johnson…

Meet Louis the Laugh – the hilarious schoolboy comedian with the world's worst parents!

978-1-78270-160-6

978-1-78270-172-9

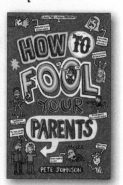

978-1-78270-247-4